D0043436

ACT

VOTE
FOR
OLIVE

BY KAYLA MILLER

HOUGHTON MIFFLIN HARCOURT
BOSTON NEW YORK

COLOR BY JESS LOME
LETTERING BY CHRIS DICKEY

hmhbooks.com

The illustrations in this book were done using inks and digital color.

Design by Andrea Miller

ISBN: 978-0-358-24218-5 hardcover
ISBN: 978-0-358-20635-4 paperback
ISBN: 978-0-358-34819-1 Barnes & Noble special edition

Manufactured in China
SCP 10 9 8 7 6 5 4 3 2 1
4500790296

FOR ALL THE TROUBLEMAKERS
AND PROBLEM SOLVERS –KM

GLUG
GLUG
GLUG

LATE FOR MY BUS. LOVE YOU GUYS. BYE!

OLIVE, HONEY, WAIT!

DON'T FORGET THE MONEY FOR YOUR FIELD TRIP.
THANKS, MOM.

MAILING SOMETHING?
NO. FIELD TRIP MONEY.

I FORGOT TO TELL MY MOM I NEEDED IT UNTIL LAST NIGHT. WE'RE LUCKY MY AUNT WAS OVER AND HAD CASH ON HER OR I MIGHT NOT BE GOING TOMORROW.

MY PARENTS MADE ME DO THE DISHES FOR A WHOLE WEEK TO "EARN" MY FIELD TRIP MONEY.
I DO THE DISHES AT MY HOUSE FOR FREE.
SAME!

I LEFT A NOTEBOOK IN THE SCIENCE LAB YESTERDAY. I WANT TO GO GET IT BEFORE CLASS STARTS. I'LL MEET YOU IN HOMEROOM!

HAVE YOU NOTICED ANYTHING DIFFERENT ABOUT HUGH LATELY?
UHH... HE GOT A HAIRCUT.

NO... THAT'S NOT IT.

LIV!
JUST THE PERSON WE WANTED TO SEE.

I KNOW! BIRD CALLS! IF YOU GET LOST, YOU CAN JUST MAKE BIRD SOUNDS AND WE'LL FIND YOU!

CAW!
KA-CAW!
TWEET!
HOO-HOO!
HOOT!
TWEET!
HOOT!

PLEASE SETTLE DOWN, EVERYONE. THIS IS A CLASSROOM, NOT AN AVIARY.

WOULD THOSE OF YOU WHO HAVE NOT YET HANDED IN THEIR PERMISSION SLIPS AND PAYMENT FOR THE FIELD TRIP TOMORROW PLEASE DO SO NOW? THIS IS THE ABSOLUTE LAST DAY THEY WILL BE ACCEPTED.

TO BEGIN TODAY'S SOCIAL STUDIES LESSON, WE'RE GOING TO BE DOING A REVIEW OF OUR SECTION ON DEMOCRACY FOR THE QUIZ THIS FRIDAY.
CAN ANYONE TELL ME WHAT A DEMOCRACY IS? ETHAN?

IT'S A TYPE OF GOVERNMENT WHERE... EVERYONE GETS TO VOTE ON EVERYTHING?

THAT'S TRUE OF ONE TYPE OF DEMOCRACY.
DOES ANYONE REMEMBER WHICH?

A DIRECT DEMOCRACY.
VERY GOOD.

IN A DIRECT DEMOCRACY, THE CITIZENS VOTE TO DECIDE ON LAWS, POLICIES, ET CETERA...
DIRECT DEMOCRACY
YES
YES
YES
NO
YES

THE MOST COMMON TYPE OF DEMOCRACY IN THE WORLD TODAY IS CALLED A REPRESENTATIVE DEMOCRACY...
WHICH MEANS...? AVA?
REPRESENTATIVE DE

THE PEOPLE VOTE TO ELECT OFFICIALS, AND THE OFFICIALS HAVE TO WORK TOGETHER TO DECIDE ON LAWS.
GOOD.

IN A REPRESENTATIVE DEMOCRACY, ELECTIONS GIVE CITIZENS A CHANCE TO VOTE FOR A PERSON—A CANDIDATE—WHO THEY THINK WILL MAKE THE BEST DECISIONS.
YES
REPRESENTATIVE DEMOCRACY
YES
YES
NO
CAT
FISH
DOG
CAT
DOG
FISH
DOG
CAT
CAT
CAT
FISH
CAT
FISH
DOG
FISH

WHICH BRINGS ME TO SOMETHING I THINK YOU'LL ALL FIND INTERESTING...
THIS SCHOOL IS A REPRESENTATIVE DEMOCRACY.

EACH YEAR, THERE IS AN ELECTION WHERE TWO STUDENTS ARE CHOSEN FROM EACH GRADE TO REPRESENT THEIR PEERS VIA THE STUDENT COUNCIL.

AS SIXTH-GRADERS, YOU ALL HAVE THE RIGHT TO VOTE IN YOUR GRADE'S ELECTION...AND TO RUN FOR OFFICE.

I'LL VOTE FOR WHOEVER CAN GET THE MOST BASKETS IN A ROW!
I WANT TO VOTE FOR YOU, ANNA.
OH MY GOSH, I WANT TO VOTE FOR YOU!
HOW ARE WE SUPPOSED TO CHOOSE WHO TO VOTE FOR?
MRS. GRIFFIN, CAN WE VOTE FOR OURSELVES?
WE SHOULD THROW A PARTY... A POLITICAL PARTY!
GET IT?
I GET IT, BUT IT'S NOT FUNNY.

WHEN I'M ELECTED PRESIDENT, SCHOOL WILL START AT NOON AND POP QUIZZES WILL BE ILLEGAL!

AND WHEN I AM ELECTED PRESIDENT, EVERY OTHER FRIDAY WILL BE BRING YOUR PET TO SCHOOL DAY!

BOYS, SIT DOWN.

THE ELECTION IS NOT FOR PRESIDENT, IT'S FOR STUDENT COUNCIL...AND WHILE YOU WILL NOT BE ABLE TO CHANGE THE HOURS OF THE SCHOOL OR ADMIT PETS, IT'S A BIG RESPONSIBILITY!

THE ELECTED INDIVIDUALS WILL ATTEND STUDENT COUNCIL MEETINGS AND BE ABLE TO DISCUSS THEIR IDEAS AND CONCERNS WITH THE FACULTY. THEY WILL BE THE VOICE OF THEIR PEERS!

NOW, PLEASE TAKE OUT YOUR WORKBOOKS.

RIIIIING!
LUNCHTIME!

BETH, COULD I SPEAK TO YOU FOR A MOMENT?
OKAY, MRS. GRIFFIN.

DO YOU WANT US TO WAIT IN THE HALL?
NO, IT'S OKAY... I'LL CATCH UP. GO GET US A GOOD TABLE.

OH! COULD YOU PASS ME A TURKEY BURGER?
UH-HUH.
I MIGHT JUST GET SALAD BAR TODAY...

THE ONLY SNACKS ARE GRAHAM CRACKERS OR PREPACKAGED APPLE SLICES AGAIN?
THIS STINKS!

I MISS THE SNACKS AT OUR OLD SCHOOL...LIKE SOFT PRETZELS—
AND CHEDDAR POPCORN—
AND STRING CHEESE—
AND **CHOCOLATE PUDDING!**

MMMMM, CHOCOLATE PUDDING!
IT'S, LIKE... BASICALLY THE PERFECT SNACK!

I FEEL LIKE THERE MUST BE A BETTER SNACK THAN PUDDING...

YEAH, SURE, PROBABLY—

BUT PUDDING IS **WAY** BETTER THAN PREPACKAGED APPLE SLICES, RIGHT?
YEAH, I'LL GIVE YOU THAT.

FRIENDS, CLASSMATES, SIXTH-GRADERS, LEND ME YOUR EARS!

FOR TOO LONG HAVE WE SUFFERED THE HUMILIATION— THE **INDIGNITY**—OF EATING LIMP, FLAVORLESS, SOGGY APPLE SLICES OUT OF A BAG!
IT'S TIME SOMEONE DID SOMETHING ABOUT IT!

BUT WHAT ARE YOU SUGGESTING TO THESE FINE PEOPLE, SAWYER? THAT WE ASK THE SCHOOL TO SERVE FRESH APPLES?
NO, TRENT, MY DEAR FRIEND... BETTER THAN THAT—

CHOCOLATE PUDDING!

SAY IT WITH US! PUD-DING, PUD-DING, PUD-DING!
PUDDING!
PUD -DING!
PUD-DING, PUD-DING, PUD-DING!

PUDDING!
PUD-DING!
VOTE TRENT AND SAWYER FOR STUDENT COUNCIL!
A VOTE FOR TRENT AND SAWYER IS A VOTE FOR PUDDING!

SAWYER, GET DOWN FROM THERE AT ONCE!

PUD-DING!
WHAT DID I MISS?
JUST THE PEASANTS REVOLTING.

IT'S FIELD TRIP DAY!

I WANT TO GO ON A FIELD TRIP!
HOP IN MY BACKPACK, GOOBER.
I'LL SNEAK YOU ONTO THE BUS.
OLIVE, DON'T ENCOURAGE HIM.

SIMON, YOUR CLASS IS GOING TO VISIT THE CRAYON FACTORY NEXT MONTH, REMEMBER?
OH YEAH!

BYE, GUYS!

EXIT
SIXTH-GRADERS GOING ON THE FIELD TRIP, PLEASE GATHER IN THE GYM!

SLAM!

IT'S IMPORTANT THAT WE ALL STICK TOGETHER WHILE WE'RE IN THE CITY TODAY, SO WE ASK THAT EVERYONE USE THE BUDDY SYSTEM.
PLEASE FORM PAIRS!
YOU'LL BE ASSIGNED A CHAPERONE AS YOU GET ON THE BUS.

OLIVE, IS IT OKAY IF I PARTNER WITH HUGH?

YEAH, THAT'S FINE. I'LL JUST PARTNER WITH AVA—

OH.

HEY, OLIVE!

WOULD YOU LIKE TO BE PARTNERS?
SURE!

IF WE'RE PARTNERS, WHO'S BUDDIES WITH BETH?

OH...SHE'S ABSENT TODAY.

BUT I SAW HER THIS MORNING.

WELL... UH...

SHE DIDN'T START FEELING SICK UNTIL WE GOT ON THE BUS. THE NURSE CALLED HER MOM TO COME PICK HER UP.
THAT STINKS! I'D HATE TO BE HOME SICK ON FIELD TRIP DAY...

THAT'S WHERE MY MOM WORKS!
CHECK OUT THAT JACKET!
THIS BIRD ISN'T EVEN AFRAID OF ME!
ATM INSIDE

OKAY, EVERYONE, FIND YOUR BUDDY...
AND STICK WITH YOUR CHAPERONE!

HUGH, WILLOW, OLIVE, CHANDA, TRENT, SAWYER, AVA, FRANNY, GRACE, AND NICK—YOU'RE ALL WITH ME! COME ALONG!

THE THEATER IS JUST UP THAT WAY.

WHAT IF THIS IS MY CHANCE TO GET NOTICED AND MAKE IT BIG?

YOU'D HAVE A BETTER SHOT OF GETTING NOTICED AT THE CIRCUS THAN THE THEATER.
BONK

PLEASE REMEMBER THIS IS A **SCHOOL** TRIP AND BEHAVE YOURSELVES ACCORDINGLY.

REVOLUTION!

GOOD FOOD DINER

AND THEN WE WENT TO THE THEATER AND THERE WERE ALL THESE OLD
POSTERS AND PHOTOS AND BACKSTAGE WE GOT TO TRY ON COSTUMES AND
GO IN THE DRESSING ROOM
BIG MIRRORS WITH LIGHTS
AND THE CREW
ORK AND THEY
OPEN AND CLOSE
REALLY
FUNNY AT
TIONS AND THEN
FIN SAID
GIRL
AGO
MILKSHAK
GROSS
I WANNA GO ON A FIELD TRIP...

I WISH EVERY DAY OF SCHOOL COULD BE A FIELD TRIP.
YEAH, YESTERDAY WAS SO FUN... I DON'T WANT TO GO BACK TO HAVING REGULAR OLD CLASSES.

THAT WAS MY FIRST TIME SEEING A REAL PLAY... I WANT TO REMEMBER IT FOREVER.

I WISH I HAD THE TICKET FOR MY SCRAPBOOK, BUT I LOST MINE...

I THINK I STILL HAVE MINE, IF YOU WANT IT.
REALLY?

THANK YOU.
DON'T MENTION IT.

HARK! WHO GOES THERE?
MRS. G

A SOLDIER OF THE KING TRYING TO INFILTRATE OUR REBEL SAFE HOUSE?!
NAY!
EAT SLEEP SKATE

I'M A REVOLUTIONARY!
HOLD, COUSIN.
METHINKS SHE TELLS THE TRUTH.
EAT SLEEP SKATE

SOOTH! I HAVE COME TO WARN YOU THAT THE KING IS ON HIS WAY!
IN FACT...
EAT

HE'S RIGHT BEHIND ME! THERE'S THE KING!
AND HE'S ACCOMPANIED BY HIS EVIL QUEEN!
EAT SLEEP SKATE

AS KING, I DECREE THAT YOU PEASANTS SHOULD STOP REBELLING AND ALSO GIVE ME ALL YOUR GOLD!

HA! THE JOKE IS ON THEE. WE PEASANTS DON'T HAVE ANY GOLD.

THEN...I SHALL TAKE ALL THINE WICKER BASKETS AND CHICKENS AND STUFF!

NOT OUR CHICKENS! ANYTHING BUT THE CHICKENS!
THIS IS THE FINAL STRAW—WE'RE TIRED OF YOUR UNJUST RULE! EN GARDE!
ALL THE CHICKENS IN THE KINGDOM WILL BE MINE!
SKATE

WHAT ARE THEY DOING?
THEY'RE JUST GOOFING ON THE PLAY FROM YESTERDAY.

OH...

THERE WILL BE NO REVOLUTIONS IN MY CLASSROOM. PLEASE TAKE YOUR SEATS.
CLINK!
CLANG!

FOR TODAY'S JOURNAL ASSIGNMENT, I'D LIKE EVERYONE TO WRITE AT LEAST TWO PAGES ON HOW SEEING THE PLAY PERFORMED ON STAGE YESTERDAY WAS DIFFERENT FROM READING ABOUT THE EVENT IN CLASS.

UMM... MRS. GRIFFIN?
YES, BETH?

I DIDN'T GO ON THE FIELD TRIP YESTERDAY, SO I HAVEN'T SEEN THE PLAY PERFORMED...

OH, THAT'S RIGHT...

HAVE YOU EVER SEEN A MOVIE BASED ON SOMETHING WE'VE COVERED IN CLASS? YOU COULD WRITE ABOUT THAT.

GIRL

NOW I WANT YOU ALL TO PRETEND YOU'RE THE FOUNDERS OF A COUNTRY, WRITING A CONSTITUTION.
WHAT DO YOU THINK IS IMPORTANT? WHAT RIGHTS SHOULD YOUR CITIZENS HAVE?

SHE EXPECTS US TO DRAFT A BILL OF RIGHTS FOR A SMALL COUNTRY? I HAD A HARD ENOUGH TIME PICKING OUT A MILKSHAKE FLAVOR AT THE DINER YESTERDAY.

IF YOU'RE NOT DRINKING A MINT CHIP MILKSHAKE, ARE YOU EVEN DRINKING A MILKSHAKE?
I WISH I COULD HAVE TRIED ALL THE FLAVORS!

UH, GUYS... WE SHOULD WORK ON THE ASSIGNMENT.

YUCK!

WHAT'S THAT?!
I THINK ONE OF MY PENS LEAKED IN MY BACKPACK... I'M GOING TO GO CLEAN IT UP IN THE BATHROOM.

I'LL MEET YOU AT LUNCH.

HUH?
SOB
HIC
SOB

HIC
SOB

UMM...
IS IT OKAY IF I COME IN?

OLIVE!

WHAT HAPPENED?

NOTHING. BETH STILL ISN'T FEELING WELL FROM YESTERDAY. WE WERE JUST—

IT'S OKAY, CHANDA.

I DON'T MIND IF OLIVE KNOWS...

I WASN'T REALLY SICK YESTERDAY...

MY FAMILY IS... ON A "TIGHT BUDGET" RIGHT NOW.

THIS MONTH MY BROTHER NEEDED NEW SOCCER CLEATS AND OUR DOG HAD TO GO TO THE VET LAST WEEK...

AND I COULD SEE HOW MUCH IT WAS STRESSING MY MOM OUT TO FIND THE MONEY TO TAKE CARE OF EVERYTHING.

I TOLD HER I COULD SKIP THE FIELD TRIP SO WE COULD SAVE THE MONEY.

I DIDN'T THINK IT WOULD BE A BIG DEAL...

BUT EVERYONE IN CLASS KEEPS TALKING ABOUT HOW MUCH FUN THEY HAD! AND I JUST FEEL...

I FEEL SO...

OH, BETH... I DIDN'T KNOW.

I'M SORRY. WHAT DID YOU DO ALL DAY WHILE WE WERE GONE?

I STILL HAD TO COME TO SCHOOL, BUT THERE WERE NO CLASSES...

THERE WERE A FEW OTHER KIDS WHO DIDN'T GO ON THE FIELD TRIP EITHER.
MAGIC
WE GOT LEFT WITH A SUBSTITUTE TEACHER...
SHE LET US WATCH MOVIES AND PLAY BOARD GAMES, SO IT WASN'T **ALL** BAD...

THAT'S STILL NOT FAIR...

YOU SHOULDN'T HAVE HAD TO MISS OUT ON THE TRIP—**NO ONE** SHOULD HAVE HAD TO MISS OUT.

THERE HAS TO BE SOMETHING SOMEONE CAN DO SO ALL THE KIDS GET TO BE INCLUDED.
MAYBE WE SHOULD TALK TO THE TEACHERS...

JUST DON'T TELL THE OTHER KIDS WHY I MISSED THE TRIP, OKAY? I DON'T WANT EVERYONE TO KNOW.

OF COURSE. IT'S OUR SECRET.

EXCUSE ME, MRS. GRIFFIN...

YES, OLIVE?
I FOUND OUT THAT SOME OF THE OTHER KIDS DIDN'T GET TO GO ON THE TRIP YESTERDAY BECAUSE THEY COULDN'T PAY THE FEE...

AND, WELL, I DON'T THINK THAT'S FAIR.

THE SCHOOL REQUIRES FAMILIES TO PAY A FEE FOR FIELD TRIPS.
THE STUDENTS WHOSE FAMILIES DON'T PAY HAVE TO STAY BEHIND.
I KNOW, BUT SOME KIDS CAN'T PAY.
CAN'T THE SCHOOL PAY FOR THOSE STUDENTS?

IT'S NOT IN THE SCHOOL'S BUDGET TO PAY FOR FIELD TRIPS WITHOUT THE HELP OF THE STUDENTS' PARENTS.

BUT WHY?

ON FIELD TRIPS, WE WANT TO GIVE YOU EXPERIENCES THAT ARE EDUCATIONAL AND MEANINGFUL... BUT THOSE EXPERIENCES COST MONEY AND, ULTIMATELY, ARE A LUXURY.

THERE HAVE BEEN YEARS WHERE THE SCHOOL HAS STRUGGLED TO FUND THE THEATER AND MUSIC PROGRAMS... AND THERE'S ALWAYS SPORTS EQUIPMENT THAT NEEDS REPLACING.

BUT WHAT IF THEY—I DON'T KNOW—CHANGED... STUFF?

OLIVE, YOU'RE RIGHT THAT IT'S NOT FAIR, BUT IT'S SIMPLY THE WAY THINGS ARE AT THE MOMENT... AND RIGHT NOW YOU'RE SUPPOSED TO BE DOING GROUP WORK.
WE CAN DISCUSS THIS MORE LATER IF YOU'D LIKE.
OKAY...

HEY, LIV!
READY TO GO?

YEAH!

BE GOOD!

OOOF!

I'M OKAY!

DO YOU GUYS HEAR THAT?
SWEET

HEY...CAN I ASK YOU GUYS SOMETHING?
SURE.
WHAT'S UP?

IF YOU ACTUALLY GET ELECTED TO THE STUDENT COUNCIL, IS THERE ANYTHING YOU'D LIKE TO CHANGE ABOUT OUR SCHOOL?

pudding PUDDING PUDDING
Pudding

I'M BEING SERIOUS.

DID YOU KNOW THAT THERE WERE SOME KIDS WHO COULDN'T AFFORD TO GO ON THE FIELD TRIP?

REALLY?
BUT I THOUGHT IT WAS ONLY, LIKE, 30 BUCKS...

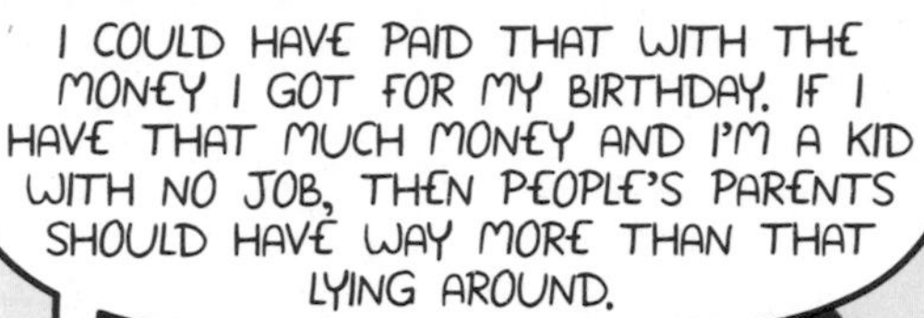

I COULD HAVE PAID THAT WITH THE MONEY I GOT FOR MY BIRTHDAY. IF I HAVE THAT MUCH MONEY AND I'M A KID WITH NO JOB, THEN PEOPLE'S PARENTS SHOULD HAVE WAY MORE THAN THAT LYING AROUND.

ADULTS HAVE TO BUY FOOD AND PAY BILLS AND STUFF... THIRTY DOLLARS CAN BE A LOT TO SOME PEOPLE.

WHAT WOULD WE BE ABLE TO DO ABOUT THAT ANYWAY?
YEAH—THAT KIND OF SEEMS LIKE A PROBLEM FOR PARENTS AND TEACHERS TO DEAL WITH...

C'MON, LIV... WE DON'T HAVE TO WORRY ABOUT MONEY!
WE'RE GOING TO BE FAMOUS PRO SKATEBOARDERS,
AND HOST A PRANK SHOW,
AND STAR IN A MOVIE,
AND RELEASE A LINE OF DESIGNER SNEAKERS!

IF WE'RE GOING TO STAR IN A MOVIE, I GET TO BE THE LEAD BECAUSE I HAVE THE BEST MOVES! THERE'S NO WAY YOU GUYS CAN KEEP UP WITH ME.
OH, YOU'RE ON! LOSER HAS TO BE THE COMIC RELIEF!

SIGH.

HEY, SUGAR. ROUGH DAY?
HEY, AUNT MOLLY.

I FOUND OUT THAT BETH COULDN'T GO ON THE FIELD TRIP BECAUSE HER PARENTS COULDN'T AFFORD IT... AND SHE SAID THERE WERE OTHER KIDS WHO WERE LEFT BEHIND TOO. IT'S NOT FAIR.

I TRIED TO TALK TO THE GUYS ABOUT IT...AND I COULD HAVE GOTTEN THEM TO CARE IF I TOLD THEM I WAS TALKING ABOUT BETH, BUT I PROMISED HER I'D KEEP IT A SECRET.

IF YOU WANT PEOPLE TO PAY MORE ATTENTION, YOU COULD ALWAYS ORGANIZE A PROTEST.

DON'T EVEN **START**, MOLLY.

I DO NOT WANT TO GET CALLS FROM OLIVE'S SCHOOL LIKE MOM USED TO GET BECAUSE OF YOUR LITTLE STUNTS.
SAVE THIS TREE
"HELLO, MA'AM,
THE FIRE DEPARTMENT IS CURRENTLY ON THE WAY TO CUT YOUR DAUGHTER LOOSE FROM THE **TREE** SHE **CHAINED HERSELF TO**."

THERE ARE PLENTY OF WAYS THAT OLIVE COULD PROTEST PEACEFULLY AND NOT GET IN ANY TROUBLE...

LIKE WHAT?

MAYBE SOME KIND OF DEMONSTRATION? WE CAN DO SOME RESEARCH TOMORROW.

PLEASE STOP RADICALIZING MY CHILDREN.

LIGHTEN UP, LU... IT'S EDUCATIONAL.

YEAH, MOM—IT'S NOT LIKE I'M GOING TO GO ON A HUNGER STRIKE OR ANYTHING!

SIGH.

YOU'RE SURE YOU DON'T MIND WATCHING THE KIDS TOMORROW?
IT'S FINE. YOU JUST WORRY ABOUT YOUR CONFERENCE THING.

SEE YOU TOMORROW.
BRIGHT AND EARLY.

GOOD LUCK, LUCY!
KNOCK 'EM DEAD, MOM!
BYE!

CHAOS REIGNS!
LET'S DIAL THAT DOWN TO "MILD PANDEMONIUM."

YUM Os

I'LL BE AT THE FRONT DESK PLANNING STORY TIME.
COME GET ME IF YOU NEED HELP FINDING ANYTHING.

I ALREADY KNOW WHAT I WANT TO READ! A BIG BOOK ABOUT BUGS!
AND I'M GOING TO DO SOME RESEARCH ON PROTESTS.

YOU GO HIT THOSE BOOKS, SUGAR...
JUST LET ME KNOW IF ANY OF THEM TRY TO HIT BACK.

TEA

VOTES FOR WOMEN
JOBS
PUBLIC SCHOOLS

END THE WAR
GAY
ERATION FRONT

OCCUPY
POWER TO THE PEOPLE
WE ARE THE 99%

WATER = LIFE

YOUTH
RIGHTS
UNITED WE STAND

HEY, OLIVE!

OLIVE, OLIVE, OLIVE, OLIVE, OLIVE, OLIVE! HEY, HEY, HEY, HEY, HEY! HEY, OLIVE, HEY, OLIVE!

DON'T YOU KNOW YOU'RE SUPPOSED TO BE QUIET IN THE LIBRARY?

I'LL BE QUIET IF YOU READ THIS TO ME.
LET ME SEE THAT.

YOU'RE OLD ENOUGH TO READ THIS ONE ON YOUR OWN, GOOB.
CHAPTER 1

I KNOW...
BUT I LIKE WHEN YOU READ TO ME AND DO FUNNY VOICES.

MY SHIFT IS OVER, NERDS. LET'S BLOW THIS POPSICLE STAND.

SO, WHERE ARE WE GOING FOR DINNER?

ACTUALLY, I'M GOING TO COOK!

ARE YOU SURE?
YEAH. I ORDERED ONE OF THOSE MEAL KIT BOXES!

THE INGREDIENTS ARE ALL MEASURED OUT AND THERE ARE INSTRUCTIONS WITH PICTURES.
I THINK I CAN HANDLE IT.

#FOOD

ANYBODY IN THE MOOD FOR SOME PB&JS?

MILK

HOW DID YOUR RESEARCH GO, SUGAR? DID YOU HAVE A PRODUCTIVE DAY?
I THINK SO... I DEFINITELY HAVE SOME IDEAS.

THE PROTESTERS I READ ABOUT WERE ALL OLDER THAN ME...AND MORE ORGANIZED...AND HAD BIG GROUPS...

WHAT IF NO ONE TAKES ME SERIOUSLY BECAUSE I'M A KID AND I'M ALONE?

YOU'RE NOT GOING TO BE ABLE TO CHANGE EVERYONE'S MIND.
THERE ARE ALWAYS GOING TO BE PEOPLE WHO WON'T LISTEN OR DON'T CARE.
BUT IF YOU CAN GET EVEN A FEW PEOPLE TO THINK ABOUT THINGS IN A DIFFERENT WAY, IT'S WORTH IT.

BUT WHAT IF **NO ONE** CARES?

SOMEONE WILL. BETH DOES. YOU DO.

IF YOU SEE SOMETHING UNFAIR AND THINK YOU CAN HELP, ALL THAT MATTERS IS THAT YOU **ACT** ON IT. THAT YOU DO SOMETHING.

KNOCK
KNOCK

MOM!

THANKS FOR TODAY.
ANYTIME. YOU KNOW THAT.

HOW DID YOUR CONFERENCE GO?
I THINK IT WENT REALLY WELL.

OLIVE! PHOOOONE!

HELLO?
OLIVE! IT'S WILLOW.
ROLL WITH IT

HUGH INVITED ME OVER AND I **NEED** YOU TO COME WITH ME...

WELL...

I'M KIND OF IN THE MIDDLE OF SOMETHING.

PLEASE, PLEASE, PLEASE, OLIVE? I REALLY WANT YOU TO BE THERE TOO! JUST SAY YES.

UM, OKAY, I GUESS... I JUST HAVE TO ASK MY MOM...

AWESOME! I'LL BE OVER IN A FEW!

DID YOU AND HUGH HAVE A FIGHT OR SOMETHING?

NO! WE'RE...FINE. IT'S— WE'RE NORMAL, REGULAR OLD HUGH AND WILLOW!

OOOKAAAY.

HERE, LET ME HELP YOU WITH THAT.
THANKS.

CAN I GET YOU GIRLS ANYTHING TO DRINK? SODA?
YEAH. THANKS.
THAT SOUNDS GREAT.

DID YOU SEE THE NEW SEASON OF **TEEN SWAMP CREATURE** IS STREAMING?
REALLY? LET'S DO A MARATHON!

HERE, WILLOW, YOU CAN HAVE THE GOOD BEANBAG CHAIR.
THANK YOU.
500

LUNCH IS READY! COME GET IT!

OH! I JUST REALIZED I DIDN'T TELL YOU GUYS YET...

TRENT AND SAWYER ASKED ME TO BE THEIR CAMPAIGN MANAGER FOR THE STUDENT COUNCIL ELECTION!

SINCE YOU'RE FRIENDS WITH THEM, WE WERE WONDERING IF YOU'D WANT TO HELP WITH THE ART FOR THEIR POSTER.

I'M KIND OF WORKING ON MY OWN PROJECT RIGHT NOW...BUT MAYBE?

I CAN HELP!

THAT'D BE AWESOME!

HEY, OLLIE!
BREE! I'M SO GLAD YOU PICKED UP!

I HAD A WEIRD DAY...
SPILL!

WILLOW AND I WENT OVER TO OUR FRIEND HUGH'S HOUSE AND SHE WAS ACTING ALL... AWKWARD.
NOT TO BE THAT GUY... BUT WILLOW **IS** AWKWARD.

YEAH...AROUND STRANGERS...
BUT SHE'S NOT USUALLY AWKWARD AROUND HUGH.

MAYBE SHE'S GOT A CRUSH.

ON HUGH?! THERE'S NO WAY! WE'VE KNOWN HIM SINCE KINDERGARTEN!

I DON'T KNOW—MY PARENTS MET IN SECOND GRADE, STARTED DATING IN HIGH SCHOOL, AND THEY'RE STILL TOGETHER. IT HAPPENS!

I DON'T WANT WILLOW AND HUGH TO START DATING!

TODAY WAS SO UNCOMFORTABLE AND BORING—THEY ONLY WANTED TO PAY ATTENTION TO EACH OTHER.

THEY CALL THAT BEING A "THIRD WHEEL."

I DON'T LIKE IT...

I COULD BE WRONG. WILLOW MIGHT BE GOING THROUGH A PHASE—OR BEING AWKWARD ABOUT SOMETHING ELSE ALTOGETHER!

HOW DO YOU THINK SHE WOULD REACT IF YOU ASKED HER AB—

HI THERE, SIMON.

GOOBER! HAVEN'T YOU EVER HEARD OF PRIVACY?

GRRRR...
HA HA HA HA

SORRY ABOUT THAT.
NO PROB.
I SHOULD SIGN OFF ANYWAY...

YEAH, ME TOO... THANKS FOR LISTENING.
KEEP ME IN THE LOOP WITH HOW THINGS WORK OUT!

YE OLDE
FOLKS' HOME

OLIVE, DEAR, HUGH AND I WANT TO SIT TOGETHER... DO YOU MIND TAKING THE **BAD** BEANBAG CHAIR?

SHRUG.

GOODBYE, CRUEL WORLD.

GOOD MORNING, OLIVE. WHAT ARE YOU UP TO?
SCIENCE

HI, GRACE.

I WANT TO PROTEST THE COST OF SCHOOL FIELD TRIPS... BUT MY MOM SAID I CAN'T DO ANYTHING THAT WOULD GET ME IN TROUBLE.

THAT MEANS NO WALKOUTS OR STRIKES.

HAVE YOU THOUGHT ABOUT DOING A PETITION?

MY AUNT STARTED A PETITION TO GET PART OF THE PARK NEAR HER HOUSE TURNED INTO A DOG PARK.
ONCE THE TOWN SAW HOW MANY PEOPLE WERE IN SUPPORT, THEY WERE WAY MORE OPEN TO THE IDEA.
SCIENCE

AND YOU CAN'T GET IN TROUBLE FOR ASKING PEOPLE TO SIGN A PAPER.
SCIENCE

STUDENTS CONCERNED ABOUT THE HIGH PRICES OF SCHOOL FIELD TRIPS

WILL YOU SIGN MY PETITION?
OF COURSE.

SIGN MY PETITION TO OPPOSE THE HIGH COST OF FIELD TRIPS?
THEY ARE GETTING MORE EXPENSIVE EVERY YEAR...

WOULD YOU LIKE TO PUT AN END TO EXCLUSIONARY FIELD TRIP COSTS?
HUH?
JUST SIGN THE PAPER.

WOULD YOU GUYS LIKE TO SIGN A PETITION TO LOWER FIELD TRIP COSTS?
SURE! SOUNDS LIKE A NOBLE CAUSE.

...14, 15, 16...

SOUR
I WANT TO TAKE MY PETITION OVER TO THE SEVENTH-GRADERS AND SEE IF I CAN GET ANY OF THEM TO SIGN.

WE SHOULD ALL GO! THEY'LL TAKE US MORE SERIOUSLY AS A GROUP.
CHIPS

UM... EXCUSE ME.

LITTLE SIXTH-GRADERS AREN'T SUPPOSED TO BE IN THIS PART OF THE CAFETERIA. WHAT DO YOU WANT?

I WAS WONDERING IF YOU'D LIKE TO SIGN MY PETITION TO LOWER THE COST THAT STUDENTS' FAMILIES HAVE TO PAY FOR THEM TO PARTICIPATE IN FIELD TRIPS?

NO.

DID YOU KNOW THAT KIDS WHO CAN'T PAY HAVE TO STAY BEHIND?

UH...DUH.

IF THEY START LOWERING THE COST OF SCHOOL TRIPS, WE'RE GOING TO END UP GOING SOMEWHERE TOTALLY BORING, LIKE ON A TOUR OF THE FIREHOUSE.

YOU DON'T THINK THAT COULD REALLY HAPPEN, DO YOU?

DO YOU REALLY THINK THE SCHOOL WOULD CANCEL THE AQUARIUM TRIP BECAUSE OF OLIVE'S PETITION?

I DON'T THINK IT MATTERS. I ONLY HAVE 25 SIGNATURES ANYWAY.

OLIVE? CAN WE TALK?

I DON'T WANT EVERYONE'S FIELD TRIPS TO GET MESSED UP.

MY MOM PROMISED ME THAT SHE'S ALREADY PUT MONEY ASIDE FOR ME TO GO TO THE AQUARIUM, SO YOU DON'T HAVE TO WORRY ABOUT IT.

I'M GLAD YOU'RE GOING TO BE ABLE TO COME...

BUT YOU SAID THERE WERE OTHER KIDS STUCK IN THE CLASSROOM WITH YOU LAST TIME.

WHAT IF THEIR PARENTS CAN'T AFFORD THE AQUARIUM TRIP EITHER?

YOU'RE RIGHT. NO ONE SHOULD HAVE TO FEEL THE WAY I DID.

EXCUSE ME, MRS. GRIFFIN...

YES, OLIVE?

I'VE STARTED A PETITION TO LOWER THE COST PARENTS HAVE TO PAY FOR FIELD TRIPS. CAN YOU GIVE IT TO THE PRINCIPAL FOR ME?

I'LL TAKE IT TO MS. LIN'S OFFICE FOR YOU AFTER CLASS.

I THINK IT'S A VERY NICE THING YOU'RE DOING, TRYING TO HELP YOUR FRIENDS.

I JUST... I DON'T WANT YOU TO GET TOO DISAPPOINTED IF THIS DOESN'T COME TO ANYTHING.

IF THIS DOESN'T WORK, I'LL TRY SOMETHING ELSE. I'LL JUST KEEP TRYING.

FIELD TRIPS SHOULD BE FREE FOR STUDENTS

SO, WHAT'S THIS ABOUT?
WE'RE TRYING TO DRAW ATTENTION TO OUR CAUSE WITH A SIT-IN.

"FIELD TRIPS SHOULD BE FREE FOR STUDENTS."
FIELD TRIPS SHOULD BE FREE FOR STUDENTS

IT'S KIND OF HARD TO READ.
AND IT SORT OF JUST LOOKS LIKE YOU'RE...SITTING.

IS THIS WHAT A SIT-IN IS SUPPOSED TO LOOK LIKE?

WELL, IN THE VIDEOS I WATCHED, THE PROTESTERS ALL HELD SIGNS AND WOULD SING OR CHANT...AND, IDEALLY, WE'D HAVE MORE PEOPLE.

I DIDN'T HAVE TIME TO COME UP WITH A SONG OR SLOGAN OR MAKE MORE SIGNS.

THE MAIN POINT IS TO SIT HERE UNTIL PEOPLE NOTICE US.

WE HAVE TO GET GOING.
BAND PRACTICE.

ARE YOU OKAY?
YEAH.

IT'S JUST THAT I THINK THIS IS IMPORTANT... AND I FEEL LIKE NO ONE IS LISTENING TO ME.

YOU NEED A WAY TO GET IN FRONT OF THE CROWD.
WHAT?

AT A GAME, IF I TRIED CHEERING FROM THE BLEACHERS, NO ONE WOULD BE ABLE TO HEAR ME...
BUT SINCE I CHEER FROM IN FRONT OF THE CROWD, THEY PAY ATTENTION.

BUT HOW CA—
AVA!
I'LL BE RIGHT THERE!

I'LL SEE YOU TOMORROW, OKAY?
YEAH...

Z
Z
Z

IT'S NOT FAIR—UNLESS WE'RE ALL THERE!
IT'S NOT FAIR—UNLESS WE'RE ALL THERE!
IT'S NOT FAIR UNLESS WE'RE ALL THERE!
FIELD TRIPS SHOULD BE AFFORDABLE
FIELD TRIPS FOR ALL

IT'S NOT FAIR—UNLESS WE'RE ALL THERE!
FIELD TRIPS SHOULD BE

IS THIS THING ON?

HEY, FRANNY, CAN YOU HELP ME WITH—

WHERE'S EVERYONE GOING?
IT'S NOT FAIR UNLESS WE'RE ALL THERE
FIELD TRIPS FOR ALL
LET'S GO TOGETHER
TRENT, SAWYER! WAIT!
BETH! AVA! COME BACK!
EVERYONE, WAIT!
IT'S NOT FAIR UNLESS WE'RE ALL THERE!
HUH?

NO, NO, NO!
NO...

WHAT'S WRONG, OLIVE?

WILLOW, YOU SHOULD SHOW OLIVE THAT DRAWING YOU DID YESTERDAY!
OKAY...

IT'S TRENT AND SAWYER!
ISN'T IT GREAT? I WANT TO USE IT ON THEIR CAMPAIGN FLYERS.

YEAH... THAT'S GREAT.

AVA!

I'VE BEEN THINKING ABOUT WHAT YOU SAID YESTERDAY AND—CAN I TALK TO YOU IN PRIVATE FOR A SECOND?
SURE.

Mrs.
G

OKAY, EVERYONE...SETTLE. I NEED TO KNOW WHO IS SERIOUS ABOUT RUNNING FOR CLASS REPRESENTATIVE.

REMEMBER, THERE IS GOING TO BE A DEBATE THIS FRIDAY. WHOEVER SIGNS UP TO HAVE THEIR NAME ON THE BALLOT WILL HAVE TO BE PREPARED TO GO ON STAGE AND ANSWER QUESTIONS FROM THEIR CLASSMATES IN FRONT OF THE ENTIRE GRADE.

WHILE TWO STUDENTS WILL BE ELECTED FROM THE SIXTH GRADE, THE SEATS WILL GO TO THE TWO CANDIDATES WITH THE MOST VOTES.

OKAY, I'LL PUT BOTH TRENT AND SAWYER DOWN AS THE CANDIDATES FOR OUR CLASS.

MOVING ON, TODAY WE'LL BE COVERING THE—
WAIT!

I'D LIKE TO RUN TOO!
BIGG DOGG

BUT, LIV...I THOUGHT YOU WERE GOING TO VOTE FOR US?
YEAH. WE EVEN TOLD HUGH WE WANTED YOU TO DO OUR CAMPAIGN POSTER!

WELL— I...

IS THIS THE SECRET PROJECT YOU SAID YOU WERE WORKING ON? WHY DIDN'T YOU JUST TELL US?

IT'S NOT— I JUST—

AS OLIVE'S CAMPAIGN MANAGER, I'D LIKE TO MAKE IT CLEAR THAT OLIVE'S DECISION TO RUN FOR STUDENT COUNCIL WAS NOT BASED ON ANY PERSONAL BIAS.

HER DECISION WAS BASED SOLELY ON HER COMMITMENT TO THE ISSUES.

IS THIS ABOUT THAT WHOLE FIELD TRIP THING?

SETTLE! QUIET, EVERYONE!

THERE WILL BE PLENTY OF TIME TO DISCUSS THIS AT THE DEBATE ON FRIDAY.

1.

TRENT, SAWYER! WAIT!

I DIDN'T MEAN TO UPSET YOU... I DIDN'T THINK YOU'D MIND IF I RAN TOO.

IT'S JUST... THIS IS SOMETHING SAWYER AND I WANTED TO DO TOGETHER.

IF **YOU** WIN ONE OF THE SPOTS, THAT MEANS ONLY ONE OF **US** WOULD BE ABLE TO BE ON THE COUNCIL.

IT DOESN'T MATTER! THERE ARE TWO SPOTS ON THE COUNCIL AND WE'RE GOING TO WIN **BOTH** OF THEM!

THAT'S ENOUGH.
COME ON, OLIVE.

DON'T WORRY ABOUT THEM. THEY'LL GET OVER THEIR **BRUISED EGOS** EVENTUALLY.

I WISH WE STILL HAD RECESS. I WOULDN'T MIND TAKING SOME OF MY FRUSTRATIONS OUT ON A KICKBALL.

OR MAYBE JUST BURYING MYSELF IN THE WOOD CHIPS UNDER THE SLIDE.
PAT PAT

HEY, OLIVE.
ARE YOU OKAY? USUALLY, WE NEVER PASS YOU.

YEAH. I JUST DIDN'T GET MUCH SLEEP LAST NIGHT.

UP LATE DOING HOMEWORK?

NO... I JUST HAD TROUBLE SLEEPING.

WE HAD BAND PRACTICE LAST NIGHT AND BY THE TIME I GOT HOME AND ATE DINNER AND SHOWERED...I HAD TO STAY UP SUPER LATE TO GET EVERYTHING FINISHED!

I TEXTED MY MOM AND SHE SAID IT'S OKAY FOR ME TO COME OVER.
AWESOME!

AVA AND I WERE GOING TO WORK ON SOME CAMPAIGN POSTERS AT MY HOUSE IF YOU WANT TO COME OVER.

I DON'T KNOW. I'M TRENT AND SAWYER'S CAMPAIGN MANAGER...

I'M SORRY, OLIVE, BUT I DON'T THINK I SHOULD.

HOW ABOUT YOU, WILLS? YOU'RE NOT TECHNICALLY PART OF TRENT AND SAWYER'S CAMP...

I **DID** DRAW THAT PICTURE FOR THEM...

I THINK I'D RATHER KEEP HELPING HUGH OUT WITH THEIR CAMPAIGN, IF THAT'S OKAY...

YEAH... IT'S OKAY.

DON'T WORRY ABOUT THEM... WE'RE THE DREAM TEAM!

SO I'M THINKING WE'LL NEED ONE BIG POSTER FOR THE CAFETERIA—
AND SMALLER ONES FOR THE HALLS AND THE CLASS BULLETIN BOARD AND—

HELLO, GIRLS. ARE YOU STAYING FOR DINNER, WILLOW?

OH—SORRY, AVA. I HEARD VOICES AND THOUGHT... WELL, NEVER MIND.
HI.

ARE **YOU** STAYING FOR DINNER, AVA?
IF IT'S NOT TOO MUCH TROUBLE...
NONE AT ALL!

WHATCHA DOIN'?
CAN I PLAY?

WE'RE NOT PLAYING.
GO BOTHER MOM—

WAIT.

HOW ARE YOU WITH
A GLUE STICK?

SIX HANDS
ARE BETTER
THAN FOUR.

I'VE BEEN THINKING...
IF IT'S NOT IN THE SCHOOL BUDGET, MAYBE WE CAN FIND A DIFFERENT WAY TO PAY FOR FIELD TRIPS WITHOUT ASKING OUR PARENTS FOR MONEY.

HOW MUCH MONEY WOULD YOU NEED?

THIRTY DOLLARS FOR EACH KID IN OUR GRADE FOR THE NEXT FIELD TRIP.

MAYBE YOU COULD ROB A BANK?

WHEN OUR CHEER SQUAD WANTED MONEY FOR NEW UNIFORMS, WE SOLD CHOCOLATE BARS.

WE HAD TO SELL BOXES AND BOXES OF THEM! BUT EVENTUALLY WE MADE ALL THE MONEY WE NEEDED.

WHERE DID YOU GET SO MANY CANDY BARS?
HONESTLY... I'M NOT REALLY SURE. THE COACHES HANDLED IT.

WHEN YOU GET ELECTED CLASS REP, YOU COULD GET THE TEACHERS TO HELP YOU SET UP A FUNDRAISER.

MAYBE... MRS. GRIFFIN SEEMS PRETTY BUSY ALREADY.

MAYBE...INSTEAD OF SELLING CANDY WE COULD... HMM...

HAVE A BAKE SALE!

WE COULD BUY EVERYTHING WE'D NEED FOR THAT RIGHT AT THE GROCERY STORE!
BUT DO YOU EVEN KNOW HOW TO BAKE?

I'M SURE I COULD FIGURE IT OUT. THEY PRINT THE DIRECTIONS RIGHT ON THE BOX!
THERE ARE INSTRUCTIONS WITH PICTURES. I THINK I CAN HANDLE IT.
#FOOD
MEAL KIT
OR WE CAN ASK FOR HELP!

I WANT BROWNIES AND COOKIES AND CUPCAKES!

WHATEVER YOU EAT, YOU HAVE TO PAY FOR—JUST LIKE EVERYONE ELSE.
BOOP

VOTE FOR OLIVE
VOTE 4 OLIVE
OLIVE BRANCHE
THE CANDIDATE WHO CARES
VOTE FOR OLIVE BRANCHE
VOTE FOR OLIVE BRANCHE
THE CANDIDATE WHO CARES
MARKERS
The Candidate who Cares!

KIDS! DINNER!

HI THERE, I'M OLIVE'S AUNT MOLLY.

NICE TO MEET YOU. I'M AVA, OLIVE'S CAMPAIGN MANAGER.

I DIDN'T REALIZE OLIVE WAS RUNNING FOR ANY POLITICAL OFFICE.
THIS IS THE FIRST I'M HEARING OF IT TOO.

OLIVE IS RUNNING FOR CLASS REPRESENTATIVE TO DRAW ATTENTION TO HER BAKE SALE INITIATIVE.
BAKE SALE INITIATIVE?

I WANT TO ORGANIZE A BAKE SALE TO HELP PAY FOR THE NEXT FIELD TRIP.
THAT WAY PARENTS WON'T HAVE TO PAY A FEE—
AND NO KIDS WILL HAVE TO STAY BEHIND AT THE SCHOOL!

THAT'S A GREAT IDEA.
I ALWAYS KNEW YOU WERE A SMART **COOKIE**.

I'M GOING TO HAVE TO MAKE SO MANY BROWNIES...

MY PARENTS CAN HELP US WITH THE BAKING AND THE COST OF SUPPLIES.
AND WE CAN SEE IF ANY OF THE OTHER KIDS IN OUR CLASS CAN HELP OUT!

I CAN MAKE SOMETHING!

OR...YOU CAN HELP WITH THE PACKAGING AND SALES!

VARSITY

FOR

WHAT'S ALL THAT?

THE CAMPAIGN POSTERS THAT AVA AND I MADE YESTERDAY!

HERE'S OUR FINISHED FLYERS! MY DAD RAN THEM OFF ON THE COPIER AT HIS OFFICE.

WE HAVE 100 COPIES!

OLIVE!

COME HERE FOR A SECOND.

LISTEN, LIV... WE'VE BEEN TALKING...
SAWYER FOR STUDENT COUNCIL!

IF YOU WANTED TO CHANGE YOUR MIND—DROP OUT OF THE RACE, ENDORSE **US**, JOIN THE **WINNING** TEAM—WE'D MAKE SURE THERE'S SOME EXTRA PUDDING IN YOUR FUTURE.

I DON'T ACCEPT BRIBES.

OLIVE!

LET'S GO HANG SOME OF THOSE BEAUTIFUL POSTERS BEFORE HOMEROOM!

OKAY.

I SAW THE BOYS THIS MORNING... THEY HAVE **100** CAMPAIGN FLYERS. HUGH HAD THEM PHOTOCOPIED.
OLIVE BRA
THE CA
WHO
AIR

SO WHAT?

OUR POSTERS ARE BIGGER AND HAVE GLITTER!
VOTE OLIVE FOR STUDENT COUNCIL

GLITTER IS PAPER'S MOST POWERFUL ALLY! THEIR BLACK-AND-WHITE COPIES DON'T STAND A CHANCE!
TRENT & SAWYER FOR STUDENT COUNCIL!
VOTE OLIVE FOR STUDENT COUNCIL

A VOTE FOR TRENT AND SAWYER IS A VOTE FOR PUDDING.

VOTE FOR US AND SUPPORT BETTER SNACKING FOR ALL.
T+S

NO, THANK YOU.
WE PLAN ON VOTING FOR OLIVE.

T+S

'B' SMART!
VOTE FOR
SAWYER
FOR STUDENT
COUNCIL!
LIVE

ATTENTION! ATTENTION, EVERYONE, QUIET DOWN.

IF WE COULD HAVE EVERYONE'S ATTENTION, PLEASE!

AS YOU ALL KNOW, WE'RE GOING TO BE VOTING FOR TWO NEW CLASS REPRESENTATIVES THIS FRIDAY.
WE'D LIKE TO GIVE YOU A CHANCE TO MEET YOUR CANDIDATES BEFORE THE DEBATE.

COULD THOSE OF YOU RUNNING FOR CLASS REPRESENTATIVE PLEASE COME FORWARD AND INTRODUCE YOURSELVES?

PLEASE TELL YOUR CLASSMATES WHY THEY SHOULD CONSIDER YOU FOR CLASS REP.

HI, I'M TRENT PHAN—
AND I'M SAWYER MOORE.

WE'RE THE BUDS LOOKING OUT FOR YOUR TASTE BUDS!
AND WE KNOW KARATE!

HELLO, EVERYONE, I'M BELINDA BLAIR.

EVERYONE SHOULD VOTE FOR ME BECAUSE MY DAD WORKS AT THE MAYOR'S OFFICE, SO I KNOW **ALL** ABOUT POLITICS.

GO, BELINDA!
YOU GOT THIS!

UHH...MY NAME IS TYLER DEWBERRY...

...

I'M RUNNING FOR CLASS REPRESENTATIVE BECAUSE I LIKE OUR SCHOOL...BUT I THINK WE CAN MAKE IT AN EVEN BETTER PLACE.

I ALREADY HAVE A PLAN TO MAKE SCHOOL TRIPS MORE AFFORDABLE TO STUDENTS BY HAVING A BAKE SALE—AND I'M SURE THERE'RE OTHER PROBLEMS WE CAN SOLVE IF WE WORK TOGETHER!

THANK YOU. WE CAN'T WAIT TO HEAR MORE FROM YOU AT THE DEBATE.

GO, OLIVE!
WHOO, LIV!

YOU GUYS ARE FROM MY CLASS! WHERE'S YOUR HOMEROOM LOYALTY?!

WE JUST THINK OLIVE WOULD MAKE A GOOD CLASS REP.

THANKS.
I CAN'T BELIEVE YOU.

EXCUSE ME, YOUNG LADY.

I'LL CATCH UP...

IS EVERYTHING OKAY?
SIGH.

THAT TEACHER TOLD ME I HAD TO GET CHANGED OR ELSE I'D GET A DETENTION FOR A "DRESS CODE VIOLATION."

I JUST DON'T GET IT!

I'VE WORN THAT SKIRT BEFORE AND IT'S NEVER BEEN AN ISSUE...

AND MY CHEER UNIFORM SKIRT IS SHORTER THAN THAT, AND WE'RE ALLOWED TO WEAR THOSE TO CLASS.

AND I DON'T THINK I'VE EVER HEARD OF A BOY GETTING CALLED INTO THE OFFICE FOR A DRESS CODE VIOLATION!

IF I GET ELECTED, I CAN BRING IT UP WITH THE STUDENT COUNCIL.

WELL, YOU HAVE MY VOTE...SO LONG AS I DON'T GET SENT TO STYLE JAIL FOR BEING A FASHION DISASTER.
MAYBE YOUR LOOK WILL SPARK A NEW TREND! GYM SHORTS CHIC!

I'VE BEEN MEANING TO TELL YOU, THE POSTERS YOU AND AVA MADE LOOK AMAZING!

DID YOU KNOW SHE'S WRITING A CHEER FOR YOU?
WHAT? REALLY, I—
GIRLS.

I'M SEEING SOME BLANK LAB REPORTS OVER HERE... MAYBE A LITTLE LESS CHATTING?
YES, MR. MOSS.
SORRY.

RIIIING!

OLIVE, COULD I SEE YOU FOR A MOMENT?

I WAS ABLE TO SPEAK WITH MS. LIN ABOUT YOUR PETITION THIS AFTERNOON...
AND THE SCHOOL SIMPLY CAN'T AFFORD TO FUND THE TRIPS ON ITS OWN.

I UNDERSTAND...

BUT I HEARD WHAT YOU SAID AT LUNCH ABOUT FUNDRAISING...

I'VE ALREADY COMMITTED TO TUTORING AND WORKING WITH THE COSTUME CREW FOR THE PLAY THIS SEMESTER...
BUT I COULD FREE UP SOME TIME NEXT SEMESTER.

I'D LIKE TO OFFER MY HELP WITH YOUR BAKE SALE.
REALLY? THAT'D BE GREAT! THANK YOU!

SEE YOU TOMORROW, OLIVE.
THANKS AGAIN!

TODAY HAS BEEN KIND OF CRAZY... DO YOU TWO WANT TO COME OVER TO MY PLACE AND PLAY SOME VIDEO GAMES?

I WAS PLANNING ON ASKING MY MOM TO DRIVE ME OVER TO SAWYER'S HOUSE...

I COULD ASK TRENT AND SAWYER IF YOU GUYS CAN COME TOO—BUT THAT WOULD KIND OF BE FRATERNIZING WITH THE ENEMY IN YOUR CASE, LIV.

I'D LOVE TO GO!
I'LL PASS...

OLIVE!

HOW DO THE POSTERS LOOK ALL HUNG UP?! DOES EVERYONE LOVE THEM?
DO THEY LIKE THE ONES I MADE BEST?

THEY LOOK GREAT, GOOB. EVEN THE ONE YOU ACCIDENTALLY GLUED THE COLORED PENCIL TO.
THAT ONE IS LIMITED EDITION!

OLIVE! LOOK!
DO YOU LIKE THEM?

WE WANTED TO SHOW EVERYONE THAT WE SUPPORT YOU!
WE COULDN'T MAKE FANCY BUTTONS LIKE BELINDA HAS...SO WE HAD TO GET A LITTLE CRAFTY.

OLIVE

FELT COOKIE PINS! I LOVE THEM SO MUCH!

THIS IS AMAZING! THANK YOU, GUYS!

DO YOU WANT ONE, EMILIE?
I DON'T KNOW... I'M NOT SURE WHO I'M GOING TO VOTE FOR YET.

MAY WE HAVE PINS?

I'M STILL VOTING FOR TRENT AND SAWYER—
BUT IT'S NOT EVERY DAY YOU SEE A COOKIE WITH YOUR FRIEND'S NAME ON IT.

RIIIING!

COME ON, COME ON, COME ON!

READY? OKAY!
VOTE FOR OLIVE BRANCHE

FROM THE O—
TO THE L—
TO THE I-V-E!
OLIVE IS THE CANDIDATE WHO CARES ABOUT YOU AND ME!
SO IF YOU NEED A HAND—
OR IF YOU'RE FEELING BLUE—
OUR GIRL, OLIVE BRANCHE, WILL BE THERE FOR YOU!

I LOOK FORWARD TO HEARING EVERYONE'S QUESTIONS AT THE DEBATE TOMORROW.
OLIVE
OLIVE
OLIVE

YEAH!
WHOOO!
GO OLIVE!
OLIVE!
OW-OW!

HA HA HA HA HA

THANKS FOR WARMING UP THE CROWD.
SK8

ATTENTION, EVERYONE!
SK8

WE COME BEARING GIFTS!
TASTE THE FUTURE!

PUD-DING!
PUD-DING!

RIIIIP

BLUB!

PUD-DING!
PUD-DING!
PUD-DING!
OLIVE
OLIVE

COME ON, LET'S GO—
OLIVE

SPLAT!
OLIVE

VOTE FOR OLIVE BRANC
THE CANDIDA WHO CARES
TRENT & SAWYER FOR STUDENT COUNCIL!
SK8
YEAH!
HA HA HA!
PUDDING!
PUDDING!
PUD-DING!

OLIVE
OLIVE

I CAN'T BELIEVE THIS!
PUDDING!
PUDDING!

YOU HAVE ABSOLUTELY NO INTEGRITY!
YOU COWARDS! I SHOULD—

WHAT'S GOING ON IN HERE?
PUD-DING!
PUDDING!
HAHAHA!
PUD-DING!
HA HAHA!

VOTE FOR BELINDA BLAIR
OH DEAR...
PUDDING!
HAHA!
PUDDING!
HA HA HA!
PUD-DING!

BOYS, THIS IS UNACCEPTABLE BEHAVIOR. YOU'LL CLEAN THIS MESS UP **THIS INSTANT!**
BUT, MRS. GRIFFIN...
WE CAN DISCUSS IT IN MS. LIN'S OFFICE ONCE YOU'RE FINISHED.

WHY DON'T YOU GIRLS SIT DOWN AND FINISH YOUR LUNCH?
OKAY...

HEY!

YOU'RE OLIVE BRANCHE, RIGHT? THE "CANDIDATE WHO CARES"?
UH, YEAH... THAT'S ME.
CAN I TALK TO YOU FOR A SECOND?
SURE.
FOR
LIVE
CANDIDATE
CARES

PROMISE NOT TO LAUGH.
I PROMISE... I DON'T FEEL LIKE **ANYTHING** COULD MAKE ME LAUGH RIGHT NOW...

SO...I'VE BEEN HAVING TROUBLE IN MATH CLASS, RIGHT?
AND I'M GETTING EXTRA HELP AND ALL THAT...
BUT SOMETIMES I STILL DO BAD ON QUIZZES.

AND THE THING IS, EVERY FRIDAY AFTER OUR QUIZ, MY MATH TEACHER MAKES US HAND OUR PAPER TO ANOTHER KID TO GRADE.

I HATE HAVING THE OTHER KIDS SEE HOW MANY QUESTIONS I GOT WRONG...

IT MAKES ME FEEL LIKE EVERYONE IN THE CLASS THINKS I'M STUPID.

IF YOU GET ELECTED TO THE STUDENT COUNCIL...DO YOU THINK YOU COULD DO SOMETHING ABOUT THAT?
I DON'T KNOW...

BUT I'D TRY.

TRYING IS GOOD ENOUGH FOR ME. YOU HAVE MY VOTE.
THANKS.

OKAY, SO I WROTE US SOME SAMPLE QUESTIONS YOU MIGHT GET ASKED TOMORROW. DO YOU KNOW WHAT YOU'RE WEARING? YOU CAN ALWAYS BORROW SOMETHING OF MINE...

ARE YOU OKAY?
YEAH.

TODAY WAS BAD... BUT IT'S OVER.

HEY, OLIVE.

HUGH IS COMING OVER TO MY HOUSE TODAY AFTER HE'S DONE HELPING TRENT AND SAWYER WITH A PROJECT.

WE'RE GOING TO PLAY **MONSTER MASHER** AND ORDER A PIZZA.

YOU SHOULD COME OVER, TOO! ESPECIALLY SINCE YOU MISSED THE FUN AT SAWYER'S YESTERDAY.

I WOULDN'T WANT TO INTERRUPT YOUR **DATE** WITH HUGH.

DATE?! HUGH AND I ARE JUST FRIENDS...

IT'S OBVIOUS YOU HAVE A CRUSH ON HIM.
I DON'T!

PUH-LEASE.

ANYONE CAN SEE THAT THE ONLY REASON YOU'RE EVEN HELPING TRENT AND SAWYER WITH THEIR CAMPAIGN IS BECAUSE HUGH IS THEIR CAMPAIGN MANAGER.

USUALLY, YOU HATE THEIR SENSE OF HUMOR!

YOU KNOW WHAT—YOU HAVEN'T BEEN **ANY** FUN LATELY!

THINGS DON'T ALWAYS HAVE TO BE FUN!

SOMETIMES THINGS ARE SERIOUS!

TRENT AND SAWYER MIGHT BE HAVING MORE FUN, BUT THEY DON'T SEEM TO GET THAT THIS MATTERS TO PEOPLE!

YOU ARE OFFICIALLY UNINVITED TO PIZZA NIGHT.

THAT'S FINE! I DON'T WANT TO HANG OUT WITH YOU ANYWAY BECAUSE I'M NOT A...A...

PUDDING BRAIN!

HEY. DID YOU WANT TO PLAY CATCH AND... TALK ABOUT IT FOR A BIT?
I'M FINE.

I HAVE TO PREPARE FOR THE DEBATE.

HOW WOULD YOU IMPROVE SCHOOL SPIRIT?
UMM... DO SOMETHING FUN TO UNITE THE STUDENTS... LIKE A CRAZY HAIR DAY?

IF YOU GET ELECTED, CAN YOU MAKE HOMEWORK ILLEGAL?

I THINK THAT MIGHT BE OUTSIDE MY JURISDICTION.

TEE
HEE

HA HA
HA
GET OUT!

IT'S ALMOST TIME FOR THE DEBATE ASSEMBLY. LET'S MOVE IN AN ORDERLY FASHION.

YOU'VE GOT THIS.
YOU CARE AND PEOPLE WILL SEE THAT.

THE WHOLE PUDDING THING MAY BE GOOD FOR A LAUGH...

BUT WHEN IT COMES DOWN TO IT, I'M SURE PEOPLE WILL VOTE FOR THE PERSON WHO HAS THEIR BEST INTERESTS IN MIND.

WELCOME TO THE SIXTH GRADE STUDENT COUNCIL DEBATE!
I'M YOUR MODERATOR, MR. MOSS.
A PUDDING IN EVERY CUP!

THE CANDIDATES WILL BE ASKED A SERIES OF QUESTIONS PREPARED BY THE STAFF BEFORE THE FLOOR IS OPENED UP TO QUESTIONS FROM STUDENTS.

TO BEGIN, I'D LIKE TO HAVE EACH CANDIDATE INTRODUCE THEMSELVES AND TALK A LITTLE ABOUT WHY THEY'RE RUNNING FOR CLASS REPRESENTATIVE.

I'M BELINDA BLAIR AND I'M RUNNING FOR STUDENT REPRESENTATIVE BECAUSE MY DAD WORKS IN LOCAL GOVERNMENT.
YOU CAN DEPEND ON ME TO BRING THE POISE AND PROFESSIONALISM OF A REAL POLITICIAN TO THE STUDENT COUNCIL!
B

I'M TRENT PHAN AND I'M RUNNING BECAUSE I'M TIRED OF EATING SOGGY, FLAVORLESS PREPACKAGED APPLE SLICES.

I'M SAWYER MOORE AND I WANT TO BRING CHOCOLATE PUDDING BACK TO THE LUNCHROOM, BABY!

HI, I'M OLIVE BRANCHE, AND I WANT TO BE A CLASS REPRESENTATIVE SO I CAN BRING ATTENTION TO THE ISSUES FACING THE STUDENT BODY.

I'M TYLER DEWBERRY...AND MY PARENTS TOLD ME I SHOULD BE IN THE DEBATE TO IMPROVE MY PUBLIC SPEAKING SKILLS...
GAME OVER

IF ELECTED TO STUDENT COUNCIL, WHAT WOULD YOUR FIRST PROPOSAL BE?

I WANT TO ADDRESS...THE BUDGET?

THE...UMM...WHAT'S IT CALLED...

THE DEFICIT!

PUD-DING!
PUDDING!
PUDDING!
PUDDING!
PUD-DING!
PUD-DING!
PUD-DING!
PUD-DING!
PUD-DING!
FAR OUT
A PUDDING IN EVERY CUP!

HA
WHOO!
PUDDING!
HA
HA
HA
HA
HA
HA
HA
YEAH!

I'D LIKE TO PROPOSE THAT WE PAY FOR SCHOOL FIELD TRIPS WITH FUNDRAISERS INSTEAD OF ASKING STUDENTS' PARENTS TO PAY OUT OF POCKET.

I...UMM... I—
GAME

I GUESS... I WOULD... WELL...

I DON'T KNOW...
GAME

IT'S OKAY, TYLER. WE CAN COME BACK TO YOU LATER, IF YOU NEED A MOMENT.

PHEW!
THANK YOU.

WHAT OTHER ISSUES WOULD YOU LIKE TO ADDRESS WHILE ON STUDENT COUNCIL?

I'D LIKE TO IMPROVE OUR SCHOOL'S IMAGE BY ACTING AS A SHINING EXAMPLE FOR OTHER STUDENTS TO LOOK UP TO.

IF SAWYER AND I ARE ELECTED, WE'D LIKE TO PERSONALLY GIVE EVERY KID IN THE GRADE A HIGH FIVE!

OR A FIST BUMP, IF THEY'D PREFER THAT!

BOOM!
FAR OUT
A PUDDING IN EVERY CUP!

I'D LIKE TO ADDRESS THE UNCLEAR DRESS CODE,
THE UNBALANCED HOMEWORK SCHEDULING THAT LEAVES STUDENTS WHO PARTICIPATE IN EXTRACURRICULARS STRUGGLING TO GET THEIR ASSIGNMENTS FINISHED,
AND THE ISSUE OF GRADE SCORE PRIVACY BETWEEN STUDENTS.

UM...
GAME OVER

I'D LIKE TO MAKE NEW FRIENDS ON THE STUDENT COUNCIL.
GAME

THE TIME HAS COME TO OPEN THE FLOOR TO STUDENT QUESTIONS.

OLIVE, HOW DO YOU PLAN ON ADDRESSING THE ISSUE OF HOMEWORK OVERSCHEDULING?

I'D ASK THE TEACHERS TO COORDINATE TO MAKE SURE NO TWO SUBJECTS HAVE BIG ASSIGNMENTS DUE ON THE SAME DAY.

MISS BLAIR, WHERE DO YOU INTEND TO CUT SPENDING, CONSIDERING ART AND THEATER TEACHERS ALREADY HAVE TO PAY FOR SOME OF THEIR OWN SUPPLIES?

THERE MUST BE EXCESS SPENDING...SOMEWHERE...

HEY, PUDDING GUYS... I DON'T LIKE CHOCOLATE PUDDING.

FAR OUT
A
PUDDING

HOW DO YOU FEEL ABOUT **BANANA** PUDDING?

THIS QUESTION IS FOR OLIVE. HOW DO YOU PLAN ON FUNDING THE FIELD TRIPS?

FOR THE AQUARIUM TRIP, I'D LIKE TO HAVE A BAKE SALE...

BUT IN THE FUTURE, IF THE SCHOOL APPROVES, WE COULD SELL CANDY BARS OR ORGANIZE A RAFFLE.

EXCUSE ME, BELINDA, BUT WHAT COLOR OF EYE SHADOW ARE YOU WEARING TODAY?
IT LOOKS AMAZING UNDER THOSE LIGHTS.

WHY, THANK YOU. IT'S MY SIGNATURE SHADE: CORALBERRY PINK.

UMM...THIS ISN'T REALLY A QUESTION...BUT WE WANTED TO TELL TYLER THAT WE HAVE A TABLETOP RPG CLUB THAT MEETS ON THURSDAYS IN THE LIBRARY IF HE WANTS TO JOIN...

THANK YOU.

ALL RIGHT, THEN, I GUESS THAT'S THE END OF THE Q AND A...

THE CANDIDATES WILL NOW MAKE THEIR CLOSING REMARKS.

VOTE FOR BELINDA BLAIR, A NATURAL-BORN LEADER.

TRENT AND I WOULD LIKE TO PRESENT OUR CLOSING STATEMENT IN THE FORM OF AN INTERPRETIVE DANCE.

FAR OUT
A PUDDING IN EVERY CUP!

HA
HA
HA
HA
HA
HA
HA
HA
HA
HA
HA
HA
HA

I KNOW EVERY STUDENT FACES THEIR OWN SPECIFIC PROBLEMS...
...AND I KNOW IT CAN BE HARD TO TALK ABOUT WHAT'S BOTHERING YOU BECAUSE IT MIGHT SEEM LIKE YOU'RE THE ONLY ONE WHO FEELS THAT WAY...
OLIVE

BUT I WANT TO LISTEN TO THOSE PROBLEMS AND HELP SOLVE THEM, IF I CAN, BECAUSE EVERY KID DESERVES TO HAVE THE BEST SCHOOL EXPERIENCE POSSIBLE.

WHOO!
YEAH!
CLAP!
CLAP!
CLAP!
CLAP!
CLAP!

THANK YOU.
CLAP!
CLAP!
PUDDING IN

UHH...I REALLY DON'T WANT TO BE ON STUDENT COUNCIL ANYMORE. I WANT TO JOIN THE RPG CLUB INSTEAD.

WELL, THAT CONCLUDES OUR DEBATE! PLEASE PLACE YOUR VOTES AS YOU ENTER THE CAFETERIA FOR LUNCH.
FAROUT
A PUDDING IN
GAME OVER

YOU ROCKED THAT! YOU HAD AN ANSWER FOR EVERY QUESTION!
STAGE

OLIVE
OLIVE

VOTE
BALLOT
BOX

VOTE
THE POLLS ARE CLOSED! WE WILL BE ANNOUNCING YOUR NEW CLASS REPRESENTATIVES AT THE END OF THE DAY.
OLIVE!
WE JUST WANTED TO LET YOU KNOW THAT WE VOTED FOR YOU.
YEAH. TWO OF OUR CLASSMATES HAD TO STAY BEHIND DURING THE LAST FIELD TRIP AND IT WAS TOTALLY UNFAIR.
WHEN YOU START ORGANIZING THE BAKE SALE, LET US KNOW. WE WANT TO GET INVOLVED!
MY ABUELITA MAKES THE **BEST** COOKIES.
THANKS, GUYS!

TAP
TAP
TAP

GUYS! PAY ATTENTION!
YOU'RE SUPPOSED TO BE PLAYING DEFENSE!

COUNT DOWN
1:45
TO END OF DAY

DON'T WORRY.
I'M SURE NO ONE VOTED FOR YOU.
YEAH—WE DIDN'T!
PLAYER'S HANDBOOK

DO YOU THINK THERE WILL BE CAMERAS?
MAYBE YOU'LL GET ON THE SCHOOL WEBSITE!

FAR OUT

WOULD THE CANDIDATES FOR THE SIXTH GRADE ELECTION PLEASE REPORT TO THE OFFICE?
Mrs.

OLIVE...CAN WE TALK TO YOU?
PLEASE?

WHAT?

WE'RE REALLY SORRY WE RUINED YOUR POSTER IN THE CAFETERIA...
BUT WE DIDN'T DO IT ON PURPOSE!

HEADS UP, DUDE!
WE WERE GOOFING AROUND AND I TOSSED A PUDDING CUP AT SAWYER—

HA!
AND I WASN'T THINKING... AND I KARATE CHOPPED IT.
I DIDN'T MEAN FOR IT TO HIT YOUR POSTER.

EVEN THOUGH IT WAS AN ACCIDENT, IT WAS STILL OUR FAULT...
WE SHOULD HAVE BEEN MORE CAREFUL. WE'RE REALLY SORRY, LIV.
OLIVE
FAR OUT

WE GOT SO INTO THIS ELECTION...
CAN WE JUST GO BACK TO BEING FRIENDS?

YEAH, I'D LIKE THAT.

YOU REALLY KNEW WHAT YOU WERE TALKING ABOUT AT THE DEBATE.
YEAH—THE ELECTION MUST BE SUPER IMPORTANT TO YOU. YOU WERE IN IT TO WIN IT!

I DUNNO... I JUST WANT TO HELP PEOPLE. GETTING ONTO THE STUDENT COUNCIL WOULD MAKE IT EASIER TO DO THAT.

NOW THAT ALL OUR CANDIDATES ARE PRESENT, IT'S TIME TO ANNOUNCE THE ELECTION RESULTS.
FAR OUT

FAR OUT

FAR OUT

IN FIFTH PLACE, WITH 10 VOTES—

SHRUG
TYLER DEWBERRY.
GAME

IN FOURTH PLACE, WITH 26 VOTES, BELINDA BLAIR.

THIS IS AN OUTRAGE!

THE LAST THREE CANDIDATES WERE VERY CLOSE IN THE POLLS.
FAR OUT

IN THIRD PLACE, WITH 42 VOTES—

OLIVE BRANCHE.

MAKING TRENT PHAN AND SAWYER MOORE THE NEW SIXTH GRADE CLASS REPRESENTATIVES, WITH 46 AND 44 VOTES RESPECTIVELY.

CONGRATS, GUYS.
OH, OLIVE...

IT'S OKAY. I'M OKAY.

BOYS, WOULD YOU LIKE TO COME SAY A FEW WORDS?
FAR OUT
MAIN OFFICE

MAIN OFFICE

VOTE
FOR
OLIVE

OLIVE!

I CAN'T BELIEVE THOSE TWO ACTUALLY PULLED IT OFF.
Mrs. G

ARE YOU OKAY?
YEAH.

I WAS JUST THINKING...
I DON'T **HAVE** TO BE ON THE STUDENT COUNCIL TO ORGANIZE A BAKE SALE.
NO, YOU DON'T.

AND I DON'T HAVE TO BE YOUR CAMPAIGN MANAGER TO HELP YOU.
FOR

WE'LL NEED TO BUY SUPPLIES, PICK A TIME AND PLACE, ADVERTISE—AND THEN ACTUALLY BAKE STUFF.
I'VE ALREADY HAD SOME FRIENDS SAY THEY WANT TO HELP AND I'M SURE WE CAN GET MORE VOLUNTEERS IF WE ASK AROUND.
AND MRS. GRIFFIN OFFERED TO LEND A HAND TOO!

HI, THIS IS TRENT. I'D LIKE TO THANK EVERYONE WHO VOTED FOR ME.
I PROMISE I'M GOING TO TRY TO GET BETTER SNACKS FOR THE LUNCHROOM. BOTH PUDDING AND FRESH FRUIT INSTEAD OF PREPACKAGED STUFF.
VOTE FOR OLIVE

AND THIS IS SAWYER. I ALSO WANT TO THANK EVERYONE FOR THEIR VOTES.
KA-CAW! KA-**CAW**!

I'LL TOTALLY GIVE EACH AND EVERY ONE OF YOU A HIGH FIVE...
VOTE FOR
HOO! HOOT!
WHAT'S THAT SOUND?

TRENT?

CHEEP, CHEEP, CHIRP!
TWEET! **TWEET!**
OLIVE

TRENT!
OLIVE!

TRENT? WHAT'S WRONG?
STOP ACTING LIKE A TOTAL BIRDBRAIN AND TELL US WHAT'S UP.

C'MON! NO TIME TO EXPLAIN.
FAR OUT

I WOULD HAVE WORN DIFFERENT SHOES IF I KNEW WE'D BE BREAKING THE "NO RUNNING IN THE HALLS" RULE.

...BUT I CAN'T ACCEPT THE STUDENT COUNCIL POSITION.

SAWYER WILL BE ACTING IN AN UNOFFICIAL CAPACITY AS MY VICE STUDENT COUNCIL MEMBER SINCE WE'VE BEEN WORKING AS A TEAM THIS WHOLE TIME ANYWAY.

WE THINK THERE'S SOMEONE ELSE WHO DESERVES TO BE ON THE STUDENT COUNCIL...

AND YOU ALL DESERVE SOMEONE LIKE HER TO BE ON YOUR STUDENT COUNCIL.

IS THIS ALLOWED, MS. LIN?
FAR OUT

I DON'T SEE WHY NOT. YOU'RE NEXT IN LINE IF MR. MOORE DOESN'T WANT HIS SEAT.

INTRODUCING YOUR NEW CLASS REP: OLIVE BRANCHE!

GO ON, LIV. GETTYSBURG ADDRESS 'EM.

I...I PROMISE TO DO MY BEST. THAT STARTS WITH ORGANIZING THE BAKE SALE TO FUND THE SPRING TRIP...
BUT IT DEFINITELY DOESN'T END THERE. THANK YOU!

CONGRATULATIONS TO TRENT AND OLIVE. CLASS IS DISMISSED FOR THE DAY.

THIS ISN'T HOW I PICTURED IT, BUT A WIN IS A WIN.
FAR OUT
OLIVE

I GUESS YOUR EGOS AREN'T AS EASILY BRUISED AS I THOUGHT.
OLIVE
OLIVE

CONGRATS, GUYS!
HOORAY FOR TRENT! HOORAY FOR SAWYER! **HOORAY FOR OLIVE!**

THREE WINNERS IN ONE CLASS? THAT HAS TO BE A RECORD.
ESPECIALLY SINCE THERE'RE ONLY TWO SPOTS.
I'M HERE TO COLLECT ON MY HIGH FIVE!
AAAAH! OLIVE!
WHOO!

SO...WE VOTED FOR YOU AFTER ALL.
WHAT? REALLY?

BUT WHICH ONE OF THE GUYS DID YOU GIVE YOUR OTHER VOTE TO?
I VOTED FOR TRENT. HUGH VOTED FOR SAWYER.

WE DREW STRAWS.

I GOT THE SHORT ONE.

DO YOU GUYS WANT TO COME OVER TODAY?
WE COULD HAVE A MOVIE MARATHON.

ACTUALLY...I WANTED TO HANG OUT WITH OLIVE TODAY—JUST THE TWO OF US.

WITH THE ELECTION AND EVERYTHING, WE HAVEN'T HAD MUCH OLIVE-WILLOW TIME.

MAYBE WE CAN ALL CHILL TOMORROW, THEN?
SOUNDS GREAT.
IT'S A PLAN!

YOU HAVE TO TELL ME ALL ABOUT THIS BAKE SALE IDEA!

DO YOU EVEN KNOW HOW TO BAKE?
WHY DO PEOPLE KEEP ASKING ME THAT?!

BAKE SALE

AKE SAL

VOTE FOR
OLIVE BRANCHE
THE CANDIDATE
WHO CARES
OLIVE

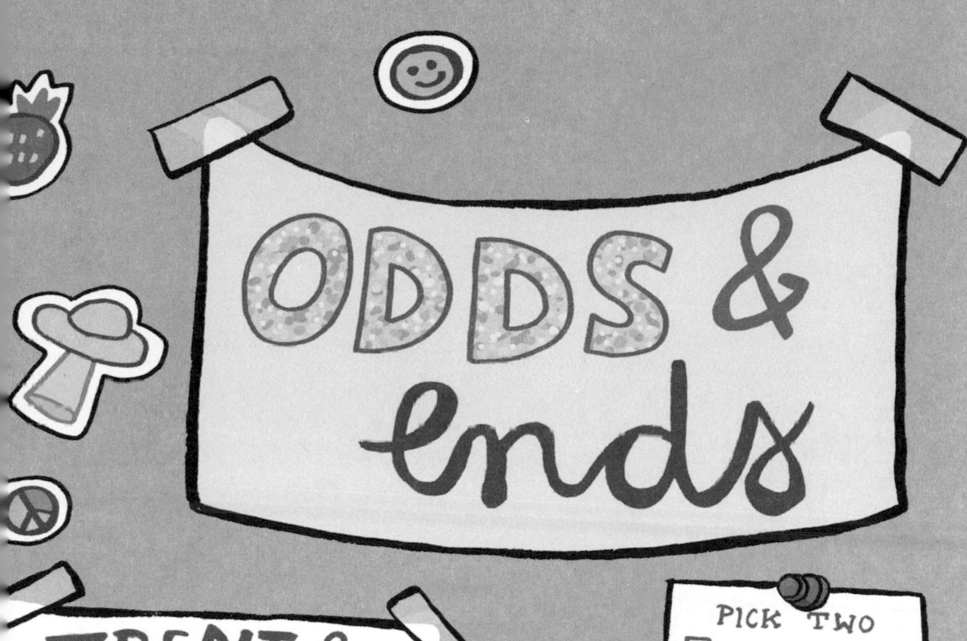
ODDS &
ends

TRENT & SAWYER
FOR STUDENT COUNCIL!

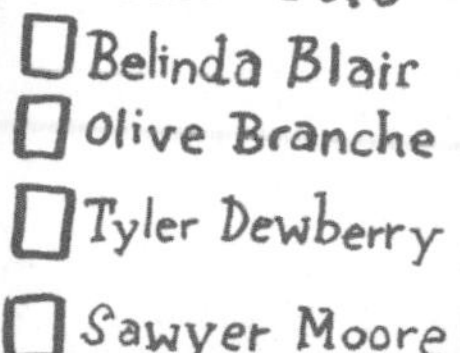
PICK TWO
Belinda Blair
Olive Branche
Tyler Dewberry

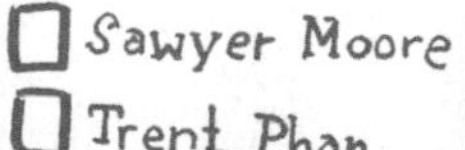
Sawyer Moore
Trent Phan

STUDENT ADMISSION
REVOLUTION!
11 AM THUR
ORCH D20
ADMISSION
REVOLUTION!
11 AM THUR
D21

TUDENTS CONCERNED
ABOUT THE HIGH
PRICES OF SCHOOL
FIELD TRIPS
Please don't
vote for m
Thank you.
-Tyler

Mint Chocolate Chip-Ins

INGREDIENTS:

½ cup (1 stick) butter, softened
¼ cup granulated sugar
¼ cup brown sugar
1 large egg
1 teaspoon vanilla extract
½ teaspoon peppermint extract
¼ teaspoon green food coloring
1½ cups flour
½ teaspoon baking powder
½ teaspoon baking soda
1 cup chocolate chips
¼ cup sprinkles
Extra sprinkles for decoration

DIRECTIONS:

1. START BY PREHEATING THE OVEN TO 350°F.
2. PREPARE YOUR BAKING SHEETS (YOU'LL PROBABLY NEED TWO) BY LINING THEM WITH PARCHMENT PAPER OR GREASING THEM WITH COOKING SPRAY OR BUTTER.
3. IN A LARGE MIXING BOWL, COMBINE THE ROOM-TEMPERATURE BUTTER, GRANULATED SUGAR, AND BROWN SUGAR. IT'S BEST TO USE A MIXER, BUT A BIG SPOON WORKS FINE IF YOU PUT A LITTLE MUSCLE BEHIND IT.

4. ADD YOUR EGG, VANILLA EXTRACT, PEPPERMINT EXTRACT, AND FOOD COLORING TO THE BUTTER AND SUGAR MIXTURE. BE SURE TO MIX WELL!

5. IN A SEPARATE BOWL, WHISK TOGETHER FLOUR, BAKING POWDER, AND BAKING SODA.

6. GRADUALLY ADD THE DRY INGREDIENTS TO THE WET INGREDIENTS AND MIX UNTIL THE DOUGH FORMS.

7. ADD CHOCOLATE CHIPS AND SPRINKLES! MIX SO THEY'RE DISTRIBUTED EVENLY THROUGHOUT. YOU WOULDN'T WANT SOMEONE TO GET A COOKIE WITH NO CHIPS!

8. FORM THE DOUGH INTO BALLS WITH ABOUT 1½ TABLESPOONS OF DOUGH IN EACH.

9. PUT THE EXTRA SPRINKLES ON A PLATE AND ROLL THE COOKIE DOUGH BALLS IN THE SPRINKLES TO COAT AT LEAST THE TOP HALF OF THE COOKIE.

10. PUT THE COOKIES ON THE BAKING SHEET 2 INCHES APART.

11. BAKE FOR 10–12 MINUTES. YOU CAN TEST TO SEE IF THE COOKIES ARE DONE BY POKING THE EDGE OF ONE WITH A SPATULA TO SEE IF IT'S FIRM.

12. REMOVE FROM THE BAKING SHEET AND LET COOL...AT LEAST A LITTLE BIT. IT'S ALWAYS A GOOD IDEA TO HAVE ONE WHILE THEY'RE STILL A LITTLE WARM.

13. SHARE AND ENJOY!

Protests of the Past

During her research sesh at the library, Olive reads about real groups throughout history who used peaceful protests to bring attention to their causes. This is by no means a comprehensive list of movements (that would take up the whole book!), but here are some brief descriptions of the protests depicted in the research montage.

Boston Tea Party

When the American colonies were formed, the colonists had to pay taxes to Britain and follow British laws, but they weren't represented in Parliament. In 1773, a group of Americans snuck onto a British ship and threw 342 crates of tea overboard as an act of rebellion against the taxation.

Suffragettes

One of the first goals of early women's rights movements was suffrage, otherwise known as the right to vote. Suffragettes circulated petitions and lobbied officials but also employed less conventional methods, such as hunger strikes and pageants. In 1893, New Zealand was the first country to give women the right to vote in national elections.

Gandhi's Salt March

In 1930, India was seeking sovereignty from British rule, and as an act of civil disobedience, protesters planned on withholding taxes, starting with the high tax on manufactured salt. Led by Gandhi, thousands of Indians donned white clothing and marched 240 miles from Ahmedabad to the coast, where they harvested their own salt.

White Rose

The White Rose was a brave group of German students who called for active resistance against Hitler and the Nazi Party during the Holocaust. They spread their message through the distribution of leaflets and use of graffiti. Some of the members were executed for their beliefs and actions.

Civil Rights

Through the 1950s and '60s, the civil rights movement in America worked toward achieving equality for Black citizens. Activists fought to end segregation, disenfranchisement, and discrimination. They utilized many methods of nonviolent protest, including sit-ins, boycotts, strikes, marches, petitions, and vigils.

Vietnam War Protests

Many Americans were unhappy with their country's involvement in the Vietnam War due to the draft, the high casualty rate, and moral reasons. Through the 1960s and early '70s, people marched in protest, organized demonstrations, and created art to express their desire for the government to end the war.

Gay Liberation Front

In 1969, the Stonewall Inn was raided by police because it catered to a primarily LGBTQ+ clientele, resulting in a riot. Following this event, the Gay Liberation Front formed to seek gay rights and equality through more peaceful means, such as marches and lobbying.

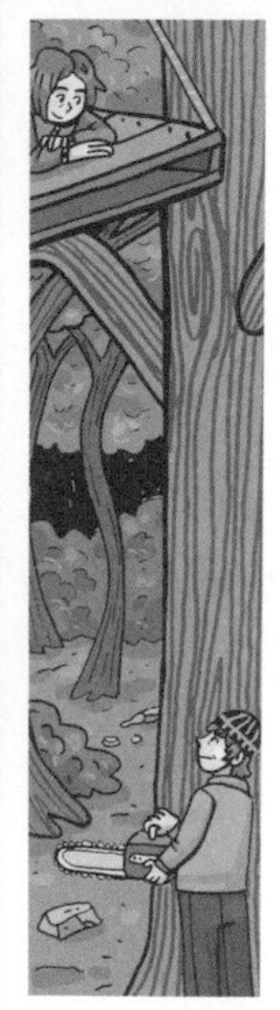

Pureora Tree Sitters

In the late 1970s, conservation activists wanted to stop the logging operations in the Pureora rainforest. They built platforms in the treetops and occupied them to protect the trees from being cut down. Their actions led to the forest becoming a protected park.

The Singing Revolution

After World War II, Estonia, Latvia, and Lithuania were incorporated into the USSR, but the nations longed for their freedom. Through the 1980s and '90s, citizens demonstrated their desire for liberation by gathering under their countries' flags and singing their national anthems along with protest songs.

The Occupy Movement

Occupy was a global movement in 2011 and 2012 concerned with the unfair economic conditions created by large corporations and the financial system. The group protested in hundreds of cities worldwide by setting up camps near and in financial districts to be a symbol of resistance and to organize with other protesters.

Pipeline Protest

In 2016, construction began on an oil pipeline that would cross beneath the Missouri River, Mississippi River, and Lake Oahe. The Standing Rock Sioux tribe and other local groups worried what the pipeline would do to these water sources. They protested by setting up camps on the land where construction was supposed to take place.

Modern Protests

Some modern protest movements build upon the achievements of past movements to advance the realization of equal rights and fair living conditions for all people. New concerns and causes, such as net neutrality and the climate crisis, also inspire people to organize and protest every day.

Suggested Reading

Below is a list of books for curious readers who want to learn more about the art of protesting, the history of protest movements, and/or how kids can make a difference.

***What Does a Protester Do?* (What Does a Citizen Do?)** written by Bridey Heing

***Protest Movements: Then and Now* (America: 50 Years of Change)** written by Eric Braun

We Rise, We Resist, We Raise Our Voices edited by Wade Hudson and Cheryl Willis Hudson

Never Too Young! 50 Unstoppable Kids Who Made a Difference written by Aileen Weintraub, illustrated by Laura Horton

Kids on Strike! written by Susan Campbell Bartoletti

***What Are Protests?* (What's the Issue?)** written by Katie Kawa

The following books focus on historical events and have details that can be upsetting. We'd recommend these for older readers or kids who have consulted with their parents.

***The Right to Protest* (American Values and Freedoms)** written by Duchess Harris, JD, PhD

Claudette Colvin: Twice Toward Justice written by Phillip Hoose

The March Trilogy written by John Lewis and Andrew Aydin, illustrated by Nate Powell

You can also ask your librarian for recommendations. I was able to read most of these titles at my local library or through interlibrary loan!

A Page From Start to Finish

THUMBNAIL

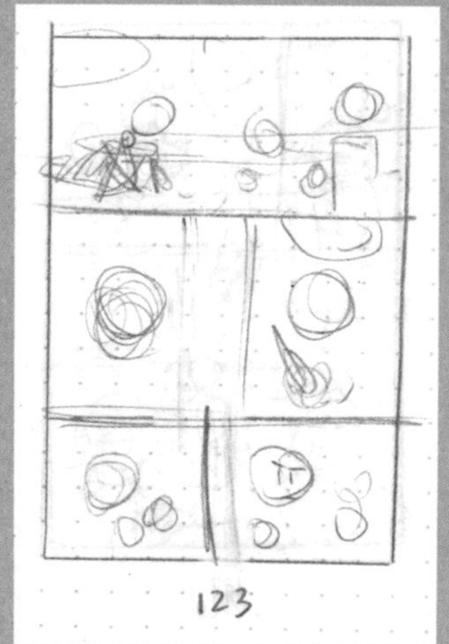

SKETCH

LETTERS

INKS

COLORS

FINAL PAGE

Acknowledgments

This book means a lot to me, and I have many people to thank for helping me make it a reality. First, I'd like to thank my editor, Mary, and my agent, Elizabeth, for their input and advice and for caring about Olive as much as I do. I look forward to our continued adventures—both literary and the lunch date variety!

Thanks to Chris for all his hard work lettering. Thanks to Andrea for not only their amazing design skills but also for being a great friend and source of support at moments when this book had run me ragged. And thanks to Jess for busting her butt to get **Act** colored and for always paying attention to the little details! I'd also like to thank Andrea's and Jess's wonderful spouses, Lor and AJ, whom I owe dinner.

Last, I'd like to thank my friends and family. Without their support, this book (and many other things in my life) would not have been possible. K, Will, and Miguel—thank you for reminding me to have fun sometimes. Dad, Mom, and Grandpa—I'm so much stronger knowing that you're always there if I need you. And of course, my Jeffrey—thank you for all you do, including being the first brave soul to taste-test my oddly colored cookie creations.

–KAYLA

Olive wants to get in on the act . . . ANY act!

Join Olive on her first adventure, available now!